*For my l[illegible]er*

First published 2022 by My Literary Adventure Inc.



This is a work of fiction and the product of the author's imagination. Any resemblance to actual persons is entirely coincidental.

My Literary Adventure Inc.
Ashford, South Australia, 5035
Phone: 61 8 8193 0450
Email: myliteraryadventure@gmail.com

| | |
|---|---|
| Creator: | Gaebler Smith, Jan, author |
| Title: | The Doors of Wisdom are Never Shut |
| ISBN: | 978-0-648 2806-9-9 |
| Fiction: | teen / adult |
| Subjects: | friendship, relationships, ageing, |

My Literary Adventure embraces the story telling culture of the original custodians of our land, the Aboriginal People.

***Read, learn, and discover your passion,***

***then follow your dreams!***

My Literary Adventure

THIS LITERARY ADVENTURE

BELONGS TO:

____________________________________

____________________________________

myliteraryadventure@gmail.com

# CONTENTS


- 'A CHEERFUL FACE IS NEARLY AS GOOD FOR AN INVALID AS HEALTHY WEATHER' .......page 9

- 'A GOOD EXAMPLE IS THE BEST SERMON' .......page 17

- 'ANY FOOL CAN CRITICIZE, CONDEMN AND COMPLAIN—AND MOST FOOLS DO' .......page 37

- 'IF YOU WOULD PERSUADE, YOU MUST APPEAL TO INTEREST RATHER THAN INTELLECT' .......page 53

- 'REMEMBER NOT ONLY TO SAY THE RIGHT THING IN THE RIGHT PLACE, BUT FAR MORE DIFFICULT STILL, TO LEAVE UNSAID THE WRONG THING AT THE TEMPTING MOMENT' .......page 65

- 'THE DOORS OF WISDOM ARE NEVER SHUT' .......page 81

# CONTENTS


- 'THE HEART OF A FOOL IS IN HIS MOUTH, BUT THE MOUTH OF A WISE MAN IS IN HIS HEART' .......page 97

- 'TO SUCCEED, JUMP AS QUICKLY AT OPPORTUNITIES AS YOU DO AT CONCLUSIONS' .......page 109

- 'WE ARE ALL BORN IGNORANT, BUT ONE MUST WORK HARD TO REMAIN STUPID' .......page 127

- 'WHAT SIGNIFIES KNOWING THE NAMES, IF YOU KNOW NOT THE NATURE OF THINGS?' .......page 137

- 'WHEN YOU'RE FINISHED CHANGING – YOU'RE FINISHED!' .......page 149

- 'WITHOUT CONTINUAL GROWTH AND PROGRESS, SUCH WORDS AS IMPROVEMENT, ACHIEVEMENT AND SUCCESS HAVE NO MEANING' .......page 159

Benjamin Franklin has influenced me throughout my life, so I think it is only fair that his meaningful quotations influence this first published selection of my short stories.

The name 'Franklin' has been with me all my life, it was the first name of my grandfather, my father and my brother.

And it is perhaps not a coincidence that after being a journalist, I also became a librarian. Benjamin Franklin, as a writer, printer and publisher is credited with initiating public libraries in Philadelphia, USA, about 300 years ago. This benefited people who would not have had access to books and who could then learn and discuss information they would never had been able to access, if the library had not been available to them.

Benjamin Franklin lived a rich and full life in England, France and America and his history, curiosity and intelligence live on in inventions (he never patented) such as bifocals, swimming fins and stoves. His signature is on the United States Declaration of Independence, he represented the United States in France during the American Revolution, and his former residence in London where he lived and worked for 16 years survives today as the very interesting Benjamin Franklin House Museum, which I was lucky to be able to visit!

Benjamin Franklin is remembered for his wit, wisdom and his writing.

I celebrate him on the following pages, using the wit and wisdom of his early quotations as my story titles... to inspire some literary adventures you will hopefully enjoy!

Writing engages a rich tapestry of ideas, memories, awareness, happiness and adventure ...and I hope these pages encourage you to write some stories, too!

*Jan Gaebler Smith*

**‘A CHEERFUL FACE IS NEARLY AS GOOD FOR AN INVALID AS HEALTHY WEATHER’**

***... Ben Franklin***

# A cheerful face is nearly as good for an invalid as healthy weather

The room was dark, not pitch black dark but that dusky dark brown that looked like the sun had just set and someone had forgotten to switch on the lights.

But the lights were now automatically switched on according to a 24 hour schedule. This innovation in the last 'upgrade' meant there were no more manual light switches. This had been applauded by management as a wonderful initiative of improving their responsibility for patient care... while Leslie had recognised that it was simply another step down into the dungeon of patient dependence.

'Most people who are here either don't know, or don't really care, whether it is night or day, so I suppose it does make things easy for the staff,' Leslie had said to herself back then when the light switches disappeared.

And she had also chided herself at the time, as simply getting what she wished for... all those years of  joking about *the lights are on, but nobody's home* when certain friends had been irritating her had now come home to roost.

Leslie considered looking for her glasses in the mound of stuff on the bedside table but lost incentive before she even made the effort. Her limbs were like lead these days. No one wanted to know about that though.

One of the most common expressions between people interacting with each other is 'How are you?' but Leslie was now very aware that no one really wants to know the answer whenever they ask that question!

Her disappointment was tempered with an awareness that came as a rude shock. *Was I equally disinterested whenever I said this?* Leslie wasn't really pleased by her answer.

'Anyway, the glasses can wait,' she mumbled aloud to herself. Her former neighbour Meredith was coming to see her today, and lawdy lawdy she sure needed her strength for that. Meredith was having lots of problems, as usual, and needed someone to confide in and it was Leslie's fortune (and more often, misfortune) that she was that trusted confidante.

Leslie also accepted she was approaching her own final curtain. She was worried what would happen to Meredith who was quite a few years younger, and also quite healthy, but also very much alone in this world. Few people really understood Meredith's neediness. She always had to be the centre of attention and star attraction and ultimately that left her with no real friends and lots of disinterested relatives. In this circumstance, for example, although Leslie was actually the one facing her final performance, Meredith was still focussed only on Meredith.

Leslie loved Meredith, but she also had to admit it really was getting more difficult to show interest and respond to Meredith's prattle as her own situation became more and more fragile.

And one of the nursing staff was a self-focussed similar type to Meredith and wearing out Leslie's patience these days, too. Thank goodness she was off today. Leslie couldn't handle them both in one day anymore!

Leslie heard footsteps approaching her room and steeled herself with a big smile for Meredith.

There was a gentle knock and then a tall figure entered the room, clearly a male stranger.

'Goodness it's dark in here! I've obviously stumbled into the wrong room but I do think you need to see the beautiful day that's outside your window!' With that, the fellow manually lifted a blind (in the process, inadvertently breaking the automatic switch that controlled it) and Leslie's heart surged.

The room transformed into shades of yellow and green and blue. Warm sunshine enveloped her bed and she saw lovely blooms in a garden bed around an oak tree. Children were playing on the lawns, while adults watched with a smile from a nearby park bench.

Leslie looked at the stranger in her room and smiled.

'Heaven can wait,' she chuckled to his cheerful face.

'Are you a doctor,' she asked him.

'Goodness no—I'm a gardener.'

**'A GOOD EXAMPLE IS THE BEST SERMON'**

... ***Ben Franklin***

## A good example is the best sermon

It was Saturday morning but Simon Simple still woke up feeling grumpy and restless, after an unusually long week in the courts. He was also feeling uneasy about that interview he'd had for *Saturday Magazine*. It wouldn't appear till next week but he suspected he was about to be crucified for his viewpoint.

Journos seemed to love highlighting how incompetent the courts were these days and aiming their sword pens at lazy lawyers, inept judges, or this or that political target.

Curiously, their emphasis was never on exploring how to *solve* the problem. Simon had a theory that the mainstream media had now evolved into the subservient puppet of the social media phenomenon that was so adept at exclaiming its anger, criticism and superiority.

'Steve Jobs was lucky he left the party when he did,' Simon mumbled to himself as he headed for his kitchen to make some breakfast.

People these days just weren't interested in exploring *why,* or thinking about *how* to change things; it was all vainglorious boasting, or protest and complain, according to Simon.

He could even track this increasing narcissistic influence on his courtroom over the last decade. Thanks to the mobile phone and social media we were now reduced to a one flick *look at me* world. This was a major concern for Simon, whenever anyone would listen. He had a little internal shudder when he remembered the reporter's raised eyebrows and excited note-taking during yesterday's interview.

'I'm getting depressed,' he chided himself, as he poured water into the kettle. Work was getting more pressured and he was having trouble adjusting to life without Rachel.

'Simple by name, simple by game—keep it simple' he recited, again, aloud. It was becoming his daily mantra.

*Judge Simple* did have a ring to it, didn't it?  He often wondered about his folks. What were they thinking, calling their kid Simon Simple?

He never got to ask the question. They were both killed in a car accident before he was old enough to understand he had a very quirky name. He'd had people trying to make him the butt of all their 'pie man' jokes all his life. And perhaps the *Simon Says* connection had subliminally made him opt for the bench. Rachel had always joked she was rather glad he opted to be a judge instead of a baker.

Now, after a long and successful career on the bench and a happy, but childless, marriage Simon was lonely and disconnected when the weekends came along; ever since Rachel had died. Saturdays had been theirs for a long lie in, then a leisurely walk, hand in hand, to their favourite coffee shop where they would chat. They had always commented about the people at other tables sitting together but not *together.* Instead those people would just be looking at their phones, notebooks or reading the Saturday papers—never talking to each other. He couldn't bear to go there for coffee now. Without Rachel to talk to anymore, he'd be reduced to being one of them, glued to his mobile or newspaper—solitude in a crowd.

Instead, he'd taken to walking along Randolph Street, close to the apartment, carrying a plastic garbage bag and one of those poles that had a 'grabit' claw at the end to easily grasp things out of reach.

Simon found it surprisingly relaxing, walking along  and letting whatever came into his mind occupy his thoughts as he picked up the multitude of rubbish scraps that had been thoughtlessly dropped and were carelessly blowing along the footpath and verge of this busy road. By his first 2000 Fitbit steps he usually had collected a full bag of litter.

More than a few years ago, Simon had protested loudly when this new technology gizmo had appeared after unwrapping a birthday present, but Rachel had insisted that he use it. She had been so worried back then, about *his* health. Now she was the one who was gone and wearing his Fitbit was one of the many ways he still kept her near.

Lately, his Saturday routine had become to get up and put on his pullover and trackies and look just like any ordinary guy with a community conscience, picking up the rubbish in his neighborhood. 'Have you heard about Judge Simple?' colleagues would joke among themselves, 'He turns into Simple Simon on weekends and becomes a dero picking up rubbish!'

Simon had heard, but he didn't really care what they said anymore, to his face, or behind his back. It was one of the benefits of his job. Over the years, as a defense lawyer, he'd had to train himself to be a man of no emotions. Then, when he was promoted to the bench with its continual degree of despair and debauchery coming before his courtroom, he had to either rise above or suffer the consequences. He'd seen so many of his colleagues become after hours alcoholics or engage in socially deviant behavior, almost as a way to make the day job more palatable for themselves. TV shows and people liked to joke about there being one degree of separation between the criminal and his lawyer, but sadly the maxim was sometimes true.

*Enough,* he told himself. 'The sun is shining, it's a nice day, time to go pick up some rubbish, me, myself and I.' The cloud that had begun overshadowing his mood suddenly dissipated as he straightened his shoulders and a spring lifted his steps as he headed out the front door of his apartment.

It didn't take long before he'd emptied two full bags of rubbish he'd collected from the street. As soon as his bag was full he'd empty its contents into one of the public refuse bins that were strategically placed as he walked along Randolph Street, giving the occasional car a wave when its driver tooted an acknowledgement of what he was doing. So many paper receipts, lolly wrappers, fast food wrappings, paper bags, coffee cup lids and used *Kleenex* that didn't make it into the many public bins provided.

Simon was always perplexed why people couldn't use these bins themselves. Was it defiance, a lack of manners, ignorance? People had so many 'causes' and 'demands' these days, yet they still couldn't make an effort to put their self-made rubbish into a bin conveniently provided for just that purpose!

After a glance at his wrist, he was impressed with the step count and felt justified about his weary legs and began looking forward to sitting down. He headed for the bench he knew was up ahead. As he got closer he noticed there was someone else already there. The fellow wore no shoes, his clothes were beyond what Simon would call 'dirty' and the smell confirmed his suspicions even before he spied the bottle covered with a brown paper bag and resting next to the man.

*Should I or shouldn't I?* A split second decision must be made.

'Nice day, today!' Simon nudged next to the fellow on the bench.

'I haven't seen a nice day in a long time.' Simon thought the voice was a bit slurred but it could have been more from lack of front teeth than the booze sitting beside him.

'That so? Well, I guess that means you've got something to look forward to for tomorrow then! What's your name?'

'Brett. Who wants to know anyway –what's your name? '

'Simon. I live around here and thought today was a good day for a walk.'

'Wait a minute! I recognise your voice. You're that judge they call Simple Simon. You let me go yesterday-what the hell! Why are you dressed like that and carrying rubbish?'

'I guess I could ask you the same thing!' Simon responded, having the first genuine chuckle he'd had all morning.

'And, let's keep the record straight, Brett. I didn't let you go. The jury of your peers did,' Simon added.

'They aint my peers, matey. Those people wouldn't give me the time of day in the street.

They'd more'n likely call the cops and get me arrested again.'

'Well, I seriously doubt that. But if they did make a call, you can bet you'd have plenty of time to be long gone before any cops showed up,' Simon laughed.

Brett looked up at him, cockeyed in the glare of the sun, with surprise. 'Now that's a strange thing for a judge to say.'

'Think so? You'd be surprised how many complaints come across my desk about cops not turning up. No fault of theirs, mind. When it comes to robbery, stabbings, traffic crashes, domestic violence, street fights... your being a dero  on a park bench is not going to figure highly on  police priorities.'

Brett reached for his bottle making a mock toast to Simon... 'You really know how to make a guy feel important.'

'We both started out as sweet little babies Brett, what happened to you along life's way?'

'Long story,' he replied.

'Looks like we've both got time for it. Let me guess, unhappy marriage in there somewhere?'

'No way, matey. I had the loveliest wife you could imagine, no disrespect to your own wife if you have one.'

'I'm a widower.'

'Well, I guess you can relate to that unbearable sadness of being, when they're not by your side anymore.'

Simon instinctively put a hand on Brett's shoulder, in agreement, and encouraging him to tell his story.

'It was a long time ago. One day I had a lovely wife and baby son. And then they were gone. We woke up in the middle of the night with the house on fire and my wife was screaming for me to go get our baby. I knew it was too late and was gripping her tight, struggling to get us out of the house but she broke away from me and that was the end of all our lives. I woke up in the hospital and I've been wishing I was dead every day since.'

'Wasn't there anyone to help you?' Simon asked. 'What about your job, friends, family? I suppose grief counselling wasn't as accessible back then as it is nowadays.'

'Oh people were there at first and everyone was saying the right things. But it doesn't take long for people to just forget dead people, they want to move on. That's when they started blaming me for using the death of my wife and son to bludge at work, and many accused me of being a coward because I ran from the fire instead of saving my family. It was all so offensive I started to drink and that just created more problems. I lost friends, then I lost my job, and after I lost my job the friends that had hung on and tried to stand by me, well they gradually dropped off as well.

'As well as grief stricken, I did became guilt ridden, too. Maybe these people were right, maybe I was a coward, I could have saved my family, and I was the bludger they were seeing. My mum and dad were heartbroken and kept trying to help me but then my mum got sick. So that's when my dad and brother started blaming me, too, for causing so much grief and trouble it caused Mum to be sick. I'm sure you know how the story goes,' he patted the bottle in the paper bag.

'It didn't take long before I was living on the street and fighting with blokes to sleep on a piece of cardboard behind the State Library at night. A lot of those blokes were like me... they'd started out on the right track but life had sideswiped them. No matter how different their stories we're all street people now—there's no going back. People look at you like you're a rat about to jump out at them.'

Brett reached for the bottle beside him, then paused, looking up at Simon. 'You didn't though.'

'I didn't what?'

'Avoid me like I was dogshit.'

'Well, it may surprise you that some people treat me that way sometimes, too, because I'm a judge. The one essential difference between you and me at the moment is you're letting yourself be a victim, Brett. I'm sorry about what's happened to you, you've had a nightmare of a life but the past is exactly that, and sadly there's no way to change it,' Simon said. 'But you can control what happens tomorrow. My suggestion is it's time to wake up from the nightmare and plan some sweeter dreams. And Brett, understand this. You're not some sort of rubbish like I've been picking up off the street today and throwing away. You are a thinking, feeling human being. It's time to stop being the victim and reclaim your right to being the master of your own fate.'

'Nice lecture matey, but it's too late for me now.' Brett again reached for his bottle but simply gave it a reassuring pat.

'Well, if you think you're dead – because that's the only time when anything is *too late*—let's go get you a job at the cemetery since you seem to want to dig your own grave. I have a mate who can help us with that.'

'I like your sense of humour, matey.' Brett looked at Simon, really looked at him.

Simon held the eye contact and suddenly realised this was the first time this man had actually engaged with another person in a long time. 'Look, I've enjoyed talking to you this morning. Let's do it again next week. I'll be out on my walk again so I'll meet you here –same time, same place—ok?'

'I can't promise that. But I'll try,' Brett said.

'That's a step in the right direction,' Simon said, nodding farewell.

As Simon walked away he felt his Rachel giving him a hug of approval. He also felt curiously excited about what tomorrow would bring.

'One degree of separation' he thought to himself.

**'ANY FOOL CAN CRITICIZE, CONDEMN AND COMPLAIN—AND MOST FOOLS DO'**

***... Ben Franklin***

# Any fool can criticize, condemn and complain—and most fools do

It had been a few years since Marylou had seen Lucille. Curiously she was feeling nervous and anxious, rather than happy and excited. After all, they had been friends for more than 50 years—where was all this nervousness coming from?

Lucille had rung her a few months ago and said she was going to be in town and would like to catch up and the two had then excitedly planned this lunch at their favourite meeting spot, *Charlie's*. Hard to believe it was still going after all these years since they had both been at University together.

Marylou told herself to stop being silly—what was she scared of? But if she was honest with herself she knew the answer to that question. While she had stayed here whiling away the years as a wife, mother (and now soon to become grandmother) and part-time assistant for her husband's finance company, Lucille had been out in the 'real world' as a journalist and theatre critic.

Lucille was renowned for her biting sarcasm, quick wit, and political activism and Marylou was very nervous that the world had now changed too much for them to see eye to eye, and agree on anything.

And yes, it was an ironic situation when one considered how the two had met.

They had both been living in the college dorm, which had a midnight curfew. Marylou had popped into the communal bathroom on their dorm floor and there was Lucille primping her fuzzy hair and applying last touches of makeup.

She smiled over to Marylou and said she was heading into the city, which was about an hour's drive from their campus.

'But it's already 10pm and you won't get back before curfew!' Marylou had exclaimed, not understanding back then that the look of alarm on her face would just make this situation worse.

Lucille, who was taller that Marylou, raised herself to a superior stance leaning against the bathroom sinks and looked down at Marylou saying, 'Well, it's characteristic of the black race to do our partying late at night.'

The two had laughed about it over the ensuing years; it was a major milestone in their forging a strong friendship, each probably for different reasons and vantage points.

Lucille had indeed managed to avoid a curfew issue that fateful night that brought them together, and she and Marylou had subsequently nodded to each other in secret silence that eventually grew into a friendship over the ensuing year, when they finally sat down and talked to each other one afternoon, after running into each other at a campus cafe.  That incidental meeting had developed into a regular catch-up and a strong friendship had then developed. Lucille left town the following year to take up a journalism scholarship. They had continued to write cards and letters to each other (as people did back in those pre-internet days) and they managed to see each other when Lucille was back home visiting her family.

Lucille was travelling here, there and everywhere while Marylou stayed put, and when they did get together they commented how they were living their lives in reverse. Marylou had never spent more than three years in one place when she was growing up, and now she hadn't moved in decades. Lucille had spent her whole childhood in the same town, and now she was the one who was constantly moving from one place to another!

It was one of those unspoken bonds that kept them close, even though apart.

Marylou had lived in New Orleans at a time when there were 'whites' and there were 'coloreds'. There were little signs on the bus that fitted over the seat rails that said 'colored only' and people would swap them back and forth between the seats depending on who was colored and who was white. Drinking fountains were labeled for colored use, as were public toilets. As a child, she took it all in her stride and still had great fun playing with the colored kids she met through her parents' servants, a maid and yardman, there was no prejudice from a child's perspective.

Then subtle moods began to change and segregation became subservient to integration. By fortunate coincidence her parents moved to another city up north about the same time a teacher at her school declared she would not be teaching a checker board, and a state trooper friend of the family was ambushed and shot in his car!

By the time Marylou met Lucille at University, Martin Luther King and the Chicago Seven had changed the world and the word *colored* had transformed to *black*.

Marylou's watch and phone were both giving her a simultaneous reminder that her lunch date with Lucille was in 30 minutes. She grabbed her purse, had one last look in the hall mirror and headed out to the car. She had asked Lucille if she could pick her up at her hotel, but Lucille said she was doing a quick interview with some guy at the university this morning so it would be easier to just meet at *Charlie's.*

As Marylou entered the crowded café, she was surprised to see Lucille already seated, sipping a wine and the rest of the bottle chilling on the table. As the two locked eyes, Lucille raised the empty wine glass and gestured to Marylou with a smile as she began to fill it with the wine.

They both gave each other a hug and then Lucille gave a big sigh. 'You look great! You are such a lucky girl!'

'Snap! I was just going to say the same to you, Marylou.'

'We'll, it's sure a crazy world we're in at the moment. I wish we could go back to our university days.'

'Oh Lucille, that might be a bit boring, because I'm sure we'd both do exactly the same things, all over again.'

'Although, maybe, just maybe, you'd give yourself a few extra hours before midnight to start your partying,' Marylou added with a laugh.

'Those days are long gone, dearie. I don't even make it to midnight on New Years' Eve anymore,' Lucille said, taking another sip of her wine.

Marylou was thankful she was always intuitive about this good friend of hers, even after all these years. Something was clearly bothering Lucille.

'So, how did the interview go this morning?'

Lucille looked at her with a knowing, appreciative smile.

'I think you already know the answer to that one, Louie! I think I'm getting too old for this game, and that's what it is nowadays, a game.'

'What do you mean?'

'Oh, people don't want to discuss ideas, or look at both sides of an issue anymore. They just want to criticise, complain, or bag the designated bad guy and then see how many likes they can accumulate from their fans. I think we should stop using the short version of fan… these people are fanatics in today's world, it makes me sad to say.'

'Yes, I kind of know what you mean. I've turned off all that social media stuff in favour of a good book, but I suppose you can't afford to do that in your line of work.'

'It's becoming a nightmare. This guy I was interviewing today was twittering away with his responses—sort of an interview of an interview pre-empting anything I might write. He obviously had been given a heads up that he and I are not on the same page.'

'Couldn't you just stop the interview?'

'We'll, at one stage I did think I might tell him I had to go vomit, but I just signed a mortgage on my city apartment so I need to keep working,' Lucille laughed.

'The good old days are long gone, though. I imagine my journalism Profs are rolling in their graves, no such thing as objectivity and giving both sides of a story at the same time anymore.'

'I'm not so sure about that, Lucille. I think objectivity is alive and well in the community that is out there talking to each other and looking each other in the face. The problem is with the medium at the moment, not the message.'

'Remember that story you told me when you first moved to New York and were living in that condo where the old guy used to spray disinfectant every time you got out of the elevator?'

'Oh yeah, Chas and Niele from southern Georgia, they ended up good friends. I haven't thought about them for years, both long gone now. Different generation, different culture and once we sat down and discussed the differences we started to understand how much we had in common.

'Gawd, Chas even ended up giving me a kiss on the cheek when I moved to the coast,' Lucille laughed.

The two friends relaxed into a catch-up camaraderie that made them both feel happy and at home with each other.

Marylou's watch and phone buzzed her simultaneously with a reminder as Lucille looked at her a bit surprised, but didn't say a word.

'Lucille, I'm going to have to get going now. I promised the kids I'd babysit while they go to one of those escape room parties for a friend's birthday.'

'Pity they didn't have those in our days, I might have decided on a different career,' Lucille laughed. She reached out and hugged her friend dearly as they rose from the table.

'I think you've changed my life today, Marylou, by reminding me about Chas and Niele.

'*Lucille's Objectivity*... has a unique ring to it, these days! Keep a watch out for my new blog,' she smiled as they both headed for the door.

As they walked away, in different directions, both were musing over the same thoughts about how very much they liked each other although they had so very different political viewpoints.

**'IF YOU WOULD PERSUADE, YOU MUST APPEAL TO INTEREST RATHER THAN INTELLECT'**

... ***Ben Franklin***

## If you would persuade, you must appeal to interest rather than intellect

Charlie Beechum knew he was lucky. He'd met the love of his life, an Australian girl, on a European holiday while still at University. All these years later, he now had a successful career, a wonderful family life in Australia, and since the kids had all grown and flown the coop, his wonderful wife was now giving him the opportunity to build his home consulting business which, after six months, was actually starting to have legs.

No thanks to the local phone company, though.

His land line to the house was full of static and dropping out.

That's why his first task of the day wasn't to cultivate that new Council client but he instead was having to waste valuable business time calling the local phone company and getting them to fix the line.

The phone picked up after three rings:

*Thank you for calling Phoncome. Our friendly customer service officer will be with you shortly. Please note your call may be recorded for training purposes. Please advise your service officer if you object to your call being recorded.*

'Good-morning *(crackling sound)* my name is Lynette (*static)* your account number please'

'2-5-3' crackling *sound continues*

'I'm sorry can you please repeat that'

'2534967'

'And your last name?'

'Beechum'

First name?

'Char *static-static'*

'Sorry, I didn't get that.'

'Charles.'

'And your mother's maiden name?'

'Johnston'

'Thank you Mr Beechum. My name is Lynette. How can I help you today?'

'I'm sure you've just heard all that crackling on my line! This has been happening on and off this week and the line has been dropping out and last month the line actually went dead for a few hours. I work from a home office, and this land line is vital to me communicating with all my customers so I'm hoping you guys can fix the line before it goes dead again.'

'Yes, I do hear all that crackling Mr Beechum! However, I'm so sorry I cannot help you. You are not our customer anymore according to my screen.'

'Come again? I've been paying the accounts you send to me every month for my phone line for years now! What do you *mean* I'm not your customer? I have monthly bank statements that show your company is regularly receiving money from me. If I'm not your customer, whose customer am I?'

'I'm sorry Mr Beechum, I can't tell you that due to our privacy policy.'

'This is ridiculous! If you say I'm not your customer, yet you won't give me the name of the company whose customer you *think* I am, then how am I going to get my phone fixed?'

'Uhhhh, is there anything else I can help you with today?'

'Yes, you can put me on to your supervisor. Maybe they can help me.'

'Hold on please.' *Wewillwewillrockyou* starts blasting into his ear, making Charlie feel even older and thinking maybe his kids were right, asking why he was still using a landline anyway.

'Mr Beechum, my supervisor is not available but I checked with someone else in the office and she confirmed we can't give out information about client companies, due to the privacy policy. These calls are monitored. I could lose my job and I really need my job.'

'Can I advise you I don't want this call monitored?'

'I'm afraid it's too late for that, Mr Beechum, it's already being recorded.'

'Is your supervisor a woman, Lynette?'

'Yes'

'Are there any men working with you, Lynette?'

'There was one, a guy named Jared, but he quit last week to work for an airline.'

'Lynette, if I told you I look like George Clooney would you give me the name of the company that can fix my account?'

'Ha ha, that's funny, Mr Beechum! My mum loves George Clooney. Also, just to reassure you, Mr Beechum, our qualified technicians are the ones who will actually fix your phone line. Our Company has the contract for all telecommunication infrastructure in the State. You simply have to report your fault first to the company that actually owns your account.'

'Now that you've brought it up Lynette, that's my problem. As far as I'm concerned you own my account. My monthly statements are telling me that you own my account. I pay money to your company to pay my account. No one has so much as whispered another name when it comes to my phone line. Can you think of a way I can get my phone fixed? I really, really need your help Lynette.'

'Uhhhh how's your day been so far, Mr Beechum?'

'My day hasn't been too bad, Lynette, until I made this call and discovered that you won't help me get my phone fixed.'

'I'm really sorry Mr Beechum, but like I said you must report the fault to your provider, and I can't tell you the name of *that* company because of our privacy policy.'

'Ok Lynette. Let's pretend I'm George Clooney again, and you pretend you're your mother.'

'Oh Mr Beechum, you are funny!'

'I'm going to offer you a coffee and you *really* need a coffee and we both want to get off the phone.

'Do you think you could give me a clue about the company's name without saying it out loud, so I can figure it out for myself?

' ...like maybe, how many letters it has and what's the first and last letter.'

**‘REMEMBER NOT ONLY TO SAY THE RIGHT THING IN THE RIGHT PLACE, BUT FAR MORE DIFFICULT STILL, TO LEAVE UNSAID THE WRONG THING AT THE TEMPTING MOMENT’**

**... *Ben Franklin***

## Remember not only to say the right thing in the right place, but far more difficult still, to leave unsaid the wrong thing at the tempting moment

Marv had sat in the new office all morning, waiting for the phone to ring. People had warned him, Melody most of all, that he was squandering everything on a pipedream. He didn't have the drive, he was lazy, he had no passion. And all he thought about was money. That's what they all thought about him.

The ex-banker in Marv surveyed his new office, taking in the new chairs, computer, office furniture, paintings and he added up the dollars to pass the time. There was no texture, ergonomics, wood hue in his life; it was all just about making the right impression for the money to start rolling in. Everybody needed insurance these days; along with coffee, death and taxes, insurance was the only other certainty. So why wasn't his phone ringing?

Melody had told him this morning she'd had enough. After that she hadn't spoken to him at all, other than when Ava was with them. With Ava, she smiled and said things like 'Ask Daddy to help you get ready for pre-school, sweetheart'. Then, when Ava couldn't see, she shot him a look that could kill.

Their baby, Connor, wasn't even a month old yet and Marv tried to give Melody some slack. After all, she had no idea what he was going through.

Marv stretched back in the ergonomic chair that the décor consultant had insisted he needed and grudgingly admitted it *was* comfortable.

The phone remained silent.

Marv did a Google search and sure enough, when he typed in 'best plant gift for new mothers' there was a great suggestion for a peace offering to take home to his wife.

The garden centre was on his way home, it was easy to park there and he could grab himself a hot dog in case Melody wasn't into making lunch.

He was looking for some 'lucky bamboo'.

He went up and down all the aisles of plants with no luck till he spotted a salesman, identifiable by the tee-shirt no one would wear in 'real life'. He was busy talking to a young couple with a kid in the seat part of the trolley. They had an assortment of small plants and shrubs in their trolley.

Marv sidled up near the wife, far enough away not to be eavesdropping but close enough to make it obvious he was waiting for advice, too. The salesman didn't give him eye contact, but Marv knew he knew he was there.

The salesman slowly and casually continued talking about the plants the couple had in their trolley, giving the couple a god's gift to gardening consultation with strings, bows and whistles. It was obvious the wife could feel Marv's impatience as the effusive salesman patently ignored the waiting Marv – she started pacing in place behind the trolley -- one foot, then the other, like an elephant, although she wasn't fat.

A lucky break! The salesman's mobile rang.

Incredibly, the salesman instantly dropped the family and their plants on the first ring to turn his undivided attention to the unknown caller, and begin yet another consultation. Bewildered, the little plant family remained in position, not even realising they were now being insulted, too. They continued waiting patiently for him to come back to discussing their plants, while the wife gave a nervous glance in Marv's direction, as if to ask if they were doing the right thing.

Enough!

Marv headed off towards the carpark with no backward glance. And no lucky bamboo.

As he settled in the car a little chill came over him as he thought about Melody.

It's that easy to walk away.

###

Melody glanced at her phone and noticed Marv was already late. Oh well, some things never change.

Despite having had two kids together, they rarely saw each other these days.

She really couldn't fathom why he'd never remarried. Once his business had taken off all those years ago, he'd set up offices interstate and never looked back. He was handsome, rich, and available. According to the kids, he had a fabulous house in his new hometown.

Melody had remarried about two years after the divorce, while their kids, Ava and Connor, were still young. Hal had been one of the single dads at the pre-school. Their kids liked each other and they'd had a comfortable, happy life for the last 20 years or so. *It wasn't really an exciting life... but does life have to be exciting?*

'Good afternoon, Madame, may I be of service? You look confused!'

'Oh, there you are!

'No, I'm just lost in thought...waiting for you to arrive! How are you Marv?'

'I'm fine Melody, but before we move on to the weather we'd better discuss why you needed to see me. I'm only in town for a quick business meeting—that's why I'm a bit late, sorry.

'And I'm on the 4 o'clock back home.

'You're looking great by the way. Life with Hal obviously suits you.'

'Thanks, and yes that sort of leads in to what I want to discuss.'

'.....that being?'

'Ava's wedding. She really wants Hal to walk her down the aisle and doesn't know how to tell you.'

'But *I'm* her father, and between me and you, *I'm* the one paying for the wedding!'

'That's unfair to Hal! He and I paid for Sally's wedding last year and it looks like there'll be one for Anne soon; she's in pretty strong with this latest fellow and he looks like a keeper.'

'Oh, then what a pity Hal's ex-wife doesn't have as much money as your ex-husband!'

'That's so totally out of line! You've gotten a few wrinkles and grey hair these past decades, but you're still selfish, thoughtless Marv, I see.

'I still don't know what I ever saw in you Marv.'

'Don't you?  Really?

'Remember that time we took the winery tour and got separated from the crowd and ended up in that dungeon where they kept all their rare wines and we were wondering what would happen if we swapped all the bottles around. The tour guide came barreling down worried we were getting into their good stuff just as we were contemplating our own kind of good stuff in the dark.'

'How can you remember that? That was ages ago, not long after *our* wedding.' Melody suppressed a giggle. 'We did have fun that weekend, didn't we?'

'Or that night we were headed to that boring dinner party and when we had to stop for a bottle of wine. I got robbed in the liquor store while you were beside yourself locked inside the car, scrambling around in the dark unable to find either your phone or car keys!'

'...now that was neither funny nor entertaining! I reckon that was the beginning of our end. I promised myself I had said *enough* for the last time, that night.'

'Well how about the night we were both lying in bed, just about to make up after yet another fight, when those drunks started banging on our bedroom windows and front door and screaming to let them in, while you were screaming to me they were going to wake up the kids.'

'I still dine out on that one. It was like a scene in the movies; both of us scared shitless, you calling 911 and the cops coming only to discover the drunks were lost houseguests of the people next door. That poor lady next door was too embarrassed to talk to me after that. I suppose I'm the same age now that she was back then.'

'Yeah, and the punchline to that story is that the kids slept right through it all.

'For me, there were fun and always exciting times, Mel. I'm sorry if you don't have happy memories of our years together. That's all I do have.

'There was nothing really wrong with us. I was stressed  and distracted setting up my business and you were stressed and worn out with the demands of being a young mum and we both gave in to the easiest option—getting divorced.'

'You can't really think that Marv!'

'Yep, I do. I'm going to grab a coffee—do you want another?'

As he walked up to the counter Melody replayed those years in her head. Yes, there had been lots of drama, laughter...and tears. *Hal never makes me cry. But he rarely makes me laugh, either.*

Marv sat back down holding a number for the staff to deliver the coffee. 'I made them give me a 10,' he smiled.

'Has Ava told you why she wants Hal, and not me, to walk her down the aisle?'

'It's just that he's been there for her, day in and day out, all these years she's been growing up, Marv. She reckons it would insult Hal, not to have him walk her down the aisle.'

'Wow. This reminds me of that saying... something about how you can always hurt your parents because you know they'll love you no matter what.'

'Oh come on Marv. Hal has been there for Ava. And his girls, Sally and Anne, have always treated her as their sister, too. The girls are Ava's bridesmaids.

'Who's the best man?'

'Connor.'

'A real family affair then.

'Melody, did you tell Ava we were meeting today?'

'No, she doesn't know. She said she's flying up to stay with you next month and didn't know how she was going to tell you. I thought I should try to help.'

She looked at his face, really looked at him, for the first time since he'd sat down talking to her and noticed he didn't look well, something different about his eyes. He had never been a fat man but he was looking very thin, too.

'Are you ok? You look a bit peaky.'

'Yeah sure I'm ok. I've just been punched in the guts a bit with this conversation, but that's ok. I'll survive and you know me, I'll always give you what you want.

'Look, I've got to head for the airport but I'll fix this with Ava. I'll think of something, and she'll get what she wants. I love her to bits.

'And thanks for the early warning. You take care of yourself, now.' He gave her a hug that took away years of separation.

While Melody sat a while longer, alone, in the coffee shop, Marv was in the taxi calling his doctor to cancel the chemo he'd scheduled to start next week. He didn't want Ava changing her mind out of sympathy.

As he got off the phone and looked out the window he thought about how maybe he should have tried harder to find that lucky bamboo all those years ago, and smiled sadly to himself.

**'THE DOORS OF WISDOM ARE NEVER SHUT'**

... ***Ben Franklin***

## The doors of wisdom are never shut

John Finch woke up gradually, listening to the birds warbling from his open window. It was a crisp, cool, early winter's morning and John tried to give himself some excuses to stay under the snug quilt. There was no need to race out of bed. He was a hobby farmer these days, retired and wifeless. Julie had left him years ago, and although he still felt an emptiness that there was no one anymore to ever say *good morning*, he'd also never felt any pangs over the ensuing years to change his status quo.

As he lay there thinking about maybe making a move to the bathroom, and then the kitchen for a wake-up coffee, he heard the faraway drone of his neighbor's tractor. Strangely, it made him feel nostalgic. He'd been driven these many years to change his arid block of farmland into the lush native garden, bird and animal sanctuary it had now become. People had laughed at him when he took on the project all those years ago and made sick jokes about his surname of Finch going to his head. Nobody in their right mind would do what he's thinking the 'experts' were all saying back then. And the criticism finally convinced Julie that he'd closed the door on wisdom, not to mention their financial survival.

It had surely cost him more than money. Lots of blood, sweat and tears were in the equation, too. He was not one to keep a tally, but his wife gave him a great farewell diatribe that itemized all the physical, mental and financial drains that his 'playtime' was creating without getting them anywhere. His mind's eye could still see the searing look on her face when he'd calmly advised 'slow and steady wins the race, love'.

Well, he was right, he did eventually win his race. But Julie was long gone, remarried and now living in New Zealand.

When they had first bought the block, decades that now seemed like light years ago, all of their friends had advised them against it.

Well, a precious few of those had still stayed in his fold and John took heart, telling himself they were indeed true friends. Now, whenever they visited he got lavished with compliments, not criticism, as they looked out his lounge room conservatory window into the surrounding lush countryside, or when they took fragrant walks along the paths teeming with native scents and showcasing native birdlife.

But the job was now done. It was one of the reasons John was having difficulty even finding the incentive to get up these mornings. Nowadays he tended to have discussions with himself, and he was realising he'd run out of things to 'do'. Somewhere along the line, he'd let himself become one-dimensional, focussed entirely on getting the farm transformed. And now he was there, he'd arrived.

His tablet on the bedstead started a little melody with an irritating diary reminder that he didn't know how to turn off. Sometimes he wished he couldn't access Wi-Fi and all its associated social media negativity now polluting society. That was a far bigger and immediate threat than the so-called climate scare mongering, in his opinion, not that anyone was listening. However, at the age of 70, he was warming to the idea of having an electronic diary to remind him about things.

He had to admit his mind wasn't the steel trap it used to be.

He reached for the noisy tablet to see what it was reminding him about and instantly found the incentive to jump out of bed. He'd entirely forgotten about the testimonial luncheon today... and he was the guest of honor!

##

John arrived at the Convention Centre with a few minutes to spare and ducked into the men's room before finding his assigned table, presumably as key speaker it would be the head table. As he entered the men's room he instantly wished it was a revolving door. Always the way, he was face to face with the last person he'd like to see – George Dirksen, in a word, insufferable.

To make matters worse, George didn't know he was insufferable, nor did he twig that no one else could stand him.

'John, John, my dear friend. I wouldn't have missed this event for anything! How marvelous to be acknowledged this way. You must be so pleased and thrilled that all the hard work has paid off. Will you be taking a rest from it all now or going on to new horizons, hey?'

'Well, George nice to see you and I….'

'YES, exactly my point,' George cut in  without missing a beat and monopolized the rest of the conversation as John took a much needed pee, washed his hands then escaped with them dripping wet. Today's correctness had wiped out paper towels and George was inconveniently monopolizing the space in front of the dryer.

John headed for the board that had the names and seating tables for the function and was quietly confident that George would not be at his table, at least.

He found his name, at Table 9, which must be the head table he decided, since he recognised all the names of patrons and officers of the regional Ecology Society, which was giving the award to him today. There was one name he didn't recognise, Tabby Catskill.

John made his way to the table and discovered the place cards with assigned seating around the table and sure enough, John *Finch* had been placed next to *Tabby Catskill. Why oh why do I agree to attend these events?* John mentally asked himself, with the associated dread, as he imagined what it was going to be like being forced into conversation with some eco-warrior blimp named Tabby Catskill.

Then, in quick succession, the Society Chair and other guests began rolling up to the table, taking their seats and making a buzz of small talk. It was a few minutes to the scheduled start when John felt someone sitting down to his right. He turned from the predictable conversation he'd been having with the Society's Patron about climate concerns and it wasn't that discussion that gave him a cold rush of air followed by a hot flush of surprise. Tabby Catskill was certainly no blimp; she was obviously the token dumb blonde at the table, from all the leers she was attracting from seated guests, including their wives.

'John Finch, and I presume from the place card that you are Tabby Catskill?' John said while extending his hand with a kindly smile.

'Oh here we go again! I see someone's having fun at our expense putting Finch and Tabby Catskill together-- do you get people making fun of your name as much as I do?' Tabby asked him, with a genuine smile, rather than irritation.

'At least it worked in my favor this time. I'm delighted to meet you John, and I am so happy the society is presenting this honour to you today. You certainly deserve it!'

'Oh, I don't know about that. I've really just been doing what I love, and what comes naturally,'

John said with an equally genuine smile, but secretly thrilled at her kind acknowledgement. It had been a tough road over the years and he had considered giving it all up, lots of times. 'And I'm also delighted to meet a kindred spirit, Tabby, who understands the fun other people sometimes have with our names, which we don't always see as being that funny!'

'Yes, well, I've had a long time to get used to it. My parents thought they were being cute by calling me Tabby, with no idea what that was going to be like in the school yard. And then it was even worse when I graduated to dating,' Tabby laughed. 'No surprises that *a rose by any other name would smell as sweet* is my favourite line from Shakespeare,' she said as she raised her glass of wine that the waiter had just poured, and offered him a toast.

'So, tell me, what brings Tabby Catskill to this table?' John asked.

'Well, it's probably not what you think,' Tabby laughed. 'I'm not from the cat protection society and I don't sell cat collars with bells that actually work! I have to confess John, despite my name or even, perhaps, in spite of my name, I don't like cats! And, as we know, feral cats are a huge problem.'

'Yes!' John agreed. 'And even domestic cats have been a problem around my place. Neighbours just don't understand and when I complain they say, *John, John, they're just doing what comes naturally.'*

John was now silently changing his tune to *Oh I'm so glad I accepted to attend this event!*

'I'll try to save my soap box for the speaker's lectern,' John smiled, gesturing to the front of the room where he would be speaking shortly. 'But people have become vested interest these days. They do all this breast beating about climate change and pontificate like experts on issues they know nothing about, yet if you point out to them that their pet cat is destroying the local environment, they look at you like you are a bully and how dare you pick on their gorgeous pussycat, who is not making any difference by killing the odd bird now and then.'

'Yes, I've had the same discussions with my neighbours. And then, when I ask them *how many cats do you think live in your neighborhood?* they give me a blank stare. And then the blank stare quickly turns into a *Tabby go home glare*, when I point out that the 200 cats living in the district can knock off a lot of bird and animal life during their weekly neighborhood prowls.'

'Yeah, totally agree,' John said, giving Tabby's wine glass a friendly 'toast' with his own. 'They say technology nowadays is making us smarter, but it's not necessarily making people wise. Can't believe when I hear people bragging about their cat killing local vermin or posting on social media a lamenting pic of the occasional dead bird that their cat brought home -- demonstrates the pet owners' ignorance more than anything else to me.'

'We'll you'll be very excited to hear about an innovation of my company,' Tabby said as she reached into her handbag for a brochure. 'We've developed a machine that can eradicate feral cats and save the local wildlife by combining technology with what we know about their nocturnal behaviors and the safest methods of poisoning the cat without putting the local animals at risk of eating poisoned cats.'

John and Tabby were still engrossed in their conversation and had to be interrupted by the Society Patron on John's left, signaling it was time for John to head up to the lectern.

There was a new spring in John's step as he headed for the lectern. As he adjusted the microphone, he decided to adlib, ahead of the prepared speech he held in his hand.

'Life is not a dress rehearsal,' he said into the microphone.

'We don't get to come back and try it all again. And the doors of wisdom are never shut. So please, always remember, doors offer us a two-way passage—in and out.  You can reject wisdom and walk out, or you can take the challenge, and walk in. I hope all of us in this room today have accepted the challenge to enter the door to our ecological wisdom.'

John's eyes rested happily on Tabby's smiling face, not even hearing the loud applause.

**'THE HEART OF A FOOL IS IN HIS MOUTH, BUT THE MOUTH OF A WISE MAN IS IN HIS HEART'**

**... *Ben Franklin***

## The heart of a fool is in his mouth, but the mouth of a wise man is in his heart

Leonard, as usual, was the last person to walk into the 9am meeting that *he* had called, and looked at the faces staring at him around the Board table.

Clare looked him dead in his eyes but with no smile or recognition. George was catching his eye while concentrating on twiddling his pen between his fingers and David looked straight at Leonard with his characteristic 'lights are on but nobody's home' expression.

Evelyn had not surfaced yet, which was indeed unusual. She was usually the first to front up at these editorial sessions, always cheerful and always offering to make the coffees from the machine that held prime position in a corner of the room.

'Before we start let me say that Evelyn is an apology for today,' George said with an unusual heavy handed determination as he glared around the table.

'And quite frankly, I doubt we'll ever be seeing her again!'

This last statement was met with a noticeable intake of breaths and suppressed gasps.

'Can you tell us why?' asked Clare, softly.

'I wish I could, but I don't know myself! She simply rang me last night and said after watching Patrick SanSimeon being interviewed on TV she's decided it's time to move on.'

'I guess she's getting jealous of him being so famous while we do all his work,' David quipped.

‘That’s very unfair, David!’ said Clare. ‘We all know what Patrick SanSimeon is really like. Personally, I can’t understand why the media is all over him, either.’

Leonard quickly interrupted. ‘On that point Clare, could you perhaps give Evelyn a call and meet with her and see if we can resolve this and keep her on the team? ’

As Clare looked over to signal that she would, Leonard was already moving on to the morning’s agenda.

It wasn’t till later that night that Clare was able to reach Evelyn and they both agreed to meet at Café Segundo for lunch the following day. Evelyn had at first been hesitant, it was, after all, their local work café and SanSimeon was known to like being a ‘presence’ there, but Clare convinced her by declaring that she was sure SanSimeon was off on an interstate talk tour.

The following day, Clare in the cafe ready and waiting, as she was with most things in life. She had booked their favourite table over by the window and was perusing the menu (which she actually already knew by heart) as Evelyn strode into the café with her usual calm, and acknowledging a few of her friends as she headed over to Clare.

They gave each other hugs and decided what they would eat and Clare went up to order for them.

As Clare then turned from the counter and headed back to their table she experienced one of the best examples of *life is what happens when you are making other plans.* Talking to Evelyn, and worse, pulling up a chair at their table, was Patrick SanSimeon. She raced back to the table and hoped Evelyn believed her pleading look that she had no idea this would happen.

'Patrick, I thought you were interstate,' Clare said straightaway to try to reinforce to Evelyn that this was definitely not a setup.

'I'm just off the plane and what a delight to see my two favourite researchers! This is a lovely coincidence because I'm just heading in to tell Leonard about an exciting new project I've signed that will involve you two, of course.'

'I saw your TV interview the other night,' Evelyn told Patrick in a level voice.

'Oh, thank you, wasn't it marvelous! I really liked Jacklyn as an interviewer, she just let me open my mouth and keep talking,' he guffawed in his characteristic boisterous voice.

'I covered so much ground talking about how I started writing the books as well as my early days as a musician, and my latest project for the Sudanese. It was a charm! She was happy for me to monopolize the interview --apparently Minnie Hobbs pulled out when she had learned I was on the panel! Fancy that, it seems appearing beside me was beneath her!

'Anyway, I never have any trouble talking about myself,' he guffawed again.

'Yes, while I was watching the show I did hear Jacklyn ask how you managed to write so many informative histories,' responded clever Evelyn, offering one of her artful statements that was actually a question.

'Oh you noticed that, did you? I thought I did a good job of quickly diverting the discussion! I gave Jacklyn a bit of *what for* afterwards, for that. Stupid bitch, why bite the hand that feeds her? I mean, yes you girls do all the research and virtually write all the books, if we are honest about it ...but research and facts don't sell my books.

'My name on the cover is what sells books!'

Both women looked at him with sympathetic smiles.

'Well, I'd better get in to see Leonard and tell him about the new project! I won't tell you girls—best to save the excitement so he can tell you all about it!

'Oh and girls, if you get a chance, do please share my interview with a line about how much you loved listening to me! It's important to keep the social media momentum going.'

As they watched him leave the café, Clare thought it was interesting how no one looked up to acknowledge his presence.

The two women looked at each other and shrugged.

'It could be worse, you know,' Clare said.

'Interesting you should say that,' Evelyn replied.

'I've decided it's time for me to answer that question you asked me earlier.

'I'm leaving because I've accepted that contract after all—the one I told you about, that I got offered last month.'

Clare clapped her hands and smiled.

'Hey author, any chance you need someone to help you with your research!'

**'TO SUCCEED, JUMP AS QUICKLY AT OPPORTUNITIES AS YOU DO AT CONCLUSIONS'**

... ***Ben Franklin***

## To succeed, jump as quickly at opportunities as you do to conclusions

There was already one empty takeaway coffee cup on Penelope Shawlins's desk.

She had fronted early to work this morning because she was nervous about the campaign presentation, but she had to admit she enjoyed the calming 7am walk in the crisp morning air with only a few bird calls interrupting her thoughts. It had been the right decision, buying her city apartment and saying goodbye to the morning rush hour.

Lester should be in soon; it was close to 9am and she was needing that extra caffeine boost, now.

She'd heard a *ping* from her phone earlier when she was doing a final edit. She had first sent him a text to bring her a skinny latte. When he didn't respond she'd sent a smiley face text. When that still didn't work, she'd sent one that just said *Please*.

The coffee from the work coffee machine was not the only thing Penelope hated about her job. Where should she start? Paul was about the worst agency boss she'd ever worked with—and there had been a few in the last 15 years! The difficult thing about Paul was that as a human being he was a great guy but to work for him, he was a total turkey. Paul was always letting the clients call all the shots--- which was the main reason Penelope was working early; to meet yet another impossible deadline, with no hope of any bonus. Paul had underquoted this job so much! Probably one night when he was out schmoozing with the boys; it might as well be a freebie. And then there was Neil, the account manager, the original Nowhere Man. Penelope didn't know why Paul carried him, but it seemed every agency she ever worked for always had the stereotype drunk like Neil lurking in the ranks. There were rumours Paul was a closet gay to Neil, who had waved his finger and labelled her a *white heterosexual middleclass feminist* in one of his recent drunken rants at the office happy hour. *Is this where the 'age of equality' was leading us?* Although the receptionists and clerk were female, Penelope was the only woman executive. The pressure of being a misfit in this agency, which was really starting to show signs of a sinking ship, kept niggling at her.

She had been the creative director here for a few years now and loved the actual 'work', she just didn't like the agency. But she had run out of places to go; one of the problems of being in a small town. That's why she had always insisted people call her Penelope, not Penny. Always keep it formal. There always was a tendency for things to get too familiar.

Lester walked in and put the new takeaway coffee on her desk. She looked up at him with her glasses dipped down on her nose, giving him her best smile. 'Ahhh, if we win an award for this campaign, I'll be sure and dedicate it to you! Meantime, take the cash out of the kitty jar and pay yourself back.'

And as he headed towards his desk, 'Also Lester, that was great work on those brochure designs. I've included them with the client briefing and would like you to attend to answer any questions, 11am in the boardroom – ok?' She had a quiet smile as she watched Lester head for his desk with his shoulders an inch higher. He was a good kid, lots of potential. If she ever found her way out of this place, she'd be sure to take Lester along, too.

When Penelope opened the boardroom door, at 11am on the dot according to her watch, she was surprised to see everyone already there, including Lester, and Neil, who was looking very sober for a change and in a suit. Penelope started feeling a bit anxious, realising this must really be some client if Paul was even insisting Neil shape up.

She looked over and locked eyes with the client, who curiously hadn't taken his eyes off her since she had walked into the room.

'Jared, this is our Creative Director, Penelope Shawlins. Although you'll be communicating with Neil in the main, of course, Penelope and her team are the brains, heheh, behind the campaign and best to let her explain the ins and outs of what they are planning for your franchise stores.'

Jared nodded hello, continuing to stare at Penelope.

His stares were hitting Penelope in her gut. *I know this guy, I've met him somewhere. Oh please God, don't let it be someone from those agency conferences back in the early days. It's all such a drunken blurr. He looks familiar but I'm sure I haven't seen ALL of him!*

Paul was sounding impatient. 'Penelope, are you ready to start your presentation?'

'Oh! Sorry! 'She grabbed her glasses and made an imaginary adjustment of her hair which was piled high on her head in a bun.'

' I'll just move up to the whiteboard and also, before I begin, I want to introduce Lester Johns, who will be explaining an important segment of the campaign, too.' Penelope looked over to a smiling Lester, who was holding his head very high.

Once she started her presentation the whole room began to hum with Penelope's contagious enthusiasm. Paul was smiling at her with unabashed pride, Neil was actually listening with interest, and Jared was responding with energetic smiles and nods, obviously inspired by the ideas being presented. Penelope was in her stride, this was the part of the job she loved, being able to create something and then share it with a responsive audience.

It was clear the campaign had passed muster and after an hour or so Paul was giving her a signal to close. Jared was obviously happy and Paul was suggesting they head off for an early lunch. Penelope could see Neil licking his lips, no doubt thinking of the cleansing ale waiting for him.

Jared looked at his watch, then at Paul. 'Paul if you don't mind, I'd like to discuss this a bit more with Penelope, one-on-one, if she has time?' He then looked directly into her eyes.

'You mean, now?' said Paul.

'Yes, if that's ok. I'd like to take Penelope over to my office.' He sent an enquiring, but confident look her way.

Penelope was starting to feel dizzy. *This guy knows we've met and wants to find out more. What'll I do? I know he likes my campaign. If I say I won't go with him, I could screw things up. But then, if I do go, that could screw things up, too.*

She looked over at Lester, who clearly saw nothing unusual happening.

Paul was looking at her as if to say GO! NOW!

Neil was getting nervous, wanting all this to end.

*Oh what the hell!* 'Sure, Jared, I've blocked out my morning for your campaign.'

'Great! And Paul, if you don't mind I'll pass on the lunch invitation and drop Penelope back here before 2pm.'

As they rode down in the lift, they kept the conversation non-descript and impersonal. Jared had told her his car was parked out front, but she was not prepared for the Bentley and chauffer that greeted her.

Penelope hadn't felt this excited in years, as she snuggled luxuriously into the leather of the back seat. She was smiling as she noticed Jared looking over at her.

'I've met you before,' he said.

'Think so?'

'Know so. There must only be one brown-eyed redhead named Penelope Shawlins in this world. You were the girl who was *independently wealthy*!'

Relief, surprise and recognition came back all at once to Penelope. 'Oh my god, you were the guy at Fernandos, all those years ago. Good thing I used my real name that night!' she said.

'Yes, we sure had a good time talking—me, you and your girlfriend.'

'That was Shirley. We used to go out once a week, having fun pretending we were someone else. We were both studying then.'

'Were did the *independently wealthy* bit come in?'

'Oh we just used to use that as a defense mechanism to stop loser guys hitting on us. Our way of telling them to buzz off, we weren't interested. But it backfired that night with you.' Penelope smiled to herself. 'Gosh, I can't believe how all this is coming back to me after so long. You came up and said *What do you girls do, are you independently wealthy or something* and we knew right away the guy we'd told that to earlier, who worked with you in the kitchen, must have run back to tell you about us. It was really funny at the time, even though it all seems a bit bizarre now, when you think about it.'

'Anyway, Jared, we had to give you points for trying and I suppose that's why we invited you to sit with us during your break... and of course you were good looking!' she laughed. After you'd left we both said you were a nice guy and reckoned we'd go back to see you again, but never did.'

'Your friend came back, but I wasn't interested.'

'REALLY! She did that? Well, I'll be. I've lost touch with her over the years.'

As Jared continued relating his memories it felt like he was describing some stranger to Penelope. 'You were so beautiful, and savvy. I'd never met such a gorgeous redhead and you had those big brown eyes—which I notice you are hiding behind thick unflattering glasses these days! Why's that?'

Yes Penelope DID remember this guy! 'Hey Jared, is that payback for when I said *if you have a nice face why hide it*, about the beard you had back then?'

'Well Penelope, you do look very different now with your hair all caged up in a bun and the nerdy glasses. I think I probably remembered your eyes when you came in the room without the glasses on, but as soon as Paul said your name, it all came back to me. It's amazing to think how that 20 minutes with you and your friend back then, changed my life.'

'Really? I don't see how!' Penelope felt like she was floating on a cloud with this guy... any minute now some thunder and rain was going to bring her back to reality.

'Well for starters, you were so confident, successful, street smart and prepared to meet the world, everything that I wasn't, back then' Jared said. I went back into the boring kitchen, looked around me and compared that with how you had just made me feel, and I thought that's the life I want. Your enthusiasm was contagious!'

'That's really, really sweet, but I don't think I can take any credit for your success, Jared!'

'Ah, but that's where you are so wrong Penelope! You opened the possibility of another world to me. And you're still doing it for others— look at your presentation today, this campaign you've developed is brilliant!'

'And getting back to business for a minute, that's one of the things I wanted to discuss with you. I'd like you to come work full time for me, Penelope. I've got lots of ideas and I've been looking for someone just like you to help me make them happen. I reckon we'd be a dynamite combination!'

'Oh Jared. That's really flattering but you're moving a bit fast for me. Let's walk through this current campaign and see if you're still happy.'

'I will be, no fear. But hey, do you mind if I call you Penny?'

'Sure... as long as you never ever come up to me and say *Penny for your thoughts!*'

Smiling to herself and thinking *this just might be my lucky day* as they made their way into Jared's office, Penelope was imagining the look on Lester's face when she told him where he was headed next.

**'WE ARE ALL BORN IGNORANT, BUT ONE MUST WORK HARD TO REMAIN STUPID'**

**... *Ben Franklin***

## We are all born ignorant, but one must work hard to remain stupid

It had been a long day driving around the Top End and the last thing Jerry decided he now needed was the enthusiastic hands up he was getting from those two blokes he met last night, enthusiastically gesturing over to him to join their group, which was already keenly perving round the pool filled with bikinis.

He shook his head with a simultaneous stab at *hello* and *goodbye*, making a hurried gesture looking at his watch indicating he was already late, and then headed in the opposite direction. Yes, on a personal level, his life could be so much better but for now Jerry couldn't complain about his swanky hotel and the shower waiting for him.

Jerry sold electronics—TVs, sound systems, the whole kit and caboodle-- and sometimes he felt like he was a dinosaur. Things were changing since the good ole days when he first started out in this business. He definitely couldn't do the 'contras' anymore, like he used to do. In his 'good old days' nobody had ever missed the odd TV or hi-fi that wasn't in the stock room, despite it being on the inventory.

Life goes on. They were still paying him well and putting him up in classy hotels like this one. One of the reasons he first got the job was because he could actually hold a conversation with someone he didn't know, and he was handsome... a lot of the buyers at the client stores have always been women.

After he had showered Jerry changed into his casual gear and headed into the hotel bar for a relaxing drink before deciding what he'd do next. A local trio was playing music softly in the background. They'd ramp it up later once the young ones started coming in but he'd move on by then.

In these environments when he was on his own Jerry always preferred a spot at the bar away from the music but with a good view of any action. He *was* getting older… but he could always be tempted. Although he never even bothered taking off the wedding band these days.

Jerry was enjoying the music and was ordering a second gin and tonic, when he felt a forceful pat on his back.

The bar tender looked over and this stranger simultaneously gave him the thumbs up for the same drink. 'I'm sure my buddy here can cover me on his tab,' he said in a tone that indicated Jerry and he were longtime friends.

The forceful pat then turned into a shoulder hug as the guy lent down and whispered in Jerry's ear…

'Hey, man, you ever get that trouble all fixed up? … It's been what—how many years?'

Well, with a leading intro like that, Jerry stayed chatting at the bar and drinking and was now sitting through the second music act, having shared food platters at the bar once they changed from drinking cocktails to wine and even having a few chuckles, although Jerry kept telling himself he really had nothing in common with this guy.

And Jerry's 'inner voice' kept telling him that it was hard to believe this jerk actually knew anything about him!

But he still kept buying the guy more drinks in the hope he'd finally blurt out what he knew, while at the same time Jerry was being very careful with his own drinking and not letting on that he had any 'secrets'.

After a few hours Jerry gave up. He told the guy he had a long drive heading south in the morning for an early appointment and had better call it a night.

Jerry paid the bill (well his work, paid) and while the other guy had never come close to what Jerry was so worried the guy actually knew about him, he still kept giving him those knowing winks and nods, even as they were shaking hands in farewell.

**

Several years later a friend would be telling Jerry a story one afternoon that would finally make him sigh with relief, but also give him a heads up on how he had been played bigtime at the bar that night.

They were having a BBQ and as he flame grilled some steaks, his friend was laughing about some guy he knew years ago who always used to get free drinks in ritzy hotels by going up to a perfect stranger and pretending he knew a secret in the other guy's life.

'Everybody's always got something to hide!' his friend laughed.

**‘WHAT SIGNIFIES KNOWING THE NAMES, IF YOU KNOW NOT THE NATURE OF THINGS?’**

**…** ***Ben Franklin***

## What signifies knowing the names, if you know not the nature of things?

The door opened and a woman in her 40s entered, wearing a jumpsuit that looked like workman's overalls, or perhaps a toddler's playsuit.

'Hi Grandma! I am working around here this week and I thought I would come to see you.'

'Oh, hello dear—which one are you again?'

'Oscar'

'That's right dear, I remember now. You were born the year all babies had to be named after famous homosexuals.'

'Grandma! You're not allowed to use that term anymore. Be sure you don't say it to anyone around here...they'll punish you.'

'I don't think there's much more they can do to me now, Oscar' she gave a strained laugh as she surveyed all the tubes into her body and straps that held her body to the chair.

'Well, this is a nice nursing home. Things could be a lot worse, Grandma.'

'Oscar,' she mused.

'You were always such a pretty little girl and I longed to put you in a lovely dress like I used to have for your mother when she was little, before this world changed forever.

'I used to secretly call you Lillie Langtry when you and I were alone together when you were little... she was a friend of Oscar Wilde, you know!'

'Oh Grandma, you know you're not allowed to distinguish between male and female any more—we're all the same now. You know that.'

'Yes...but Oscar, it must be so boring for people these days?

'Everybody now having to be the same as everyone else. There's no independence, no learning, no competition, no chance to shine... it all seems so colorless to me.'

'Stop Grandma! You are talking in android frequency and I don't understand any of what you just said.'

Oscar was getting frustrated but then, Grandma *was* old.

'Well Oscar, I'm so sorry you don't understand me. Last century—so many years ago, kids played with all the neighborhood kids on the street, we sat at the table and had family conversations during our evening meal and we were oh so proud of our parents. We listened to radio and watched TV programs that were about families, corny humour and moral values.

'In the 1960s Barbra Streisand was a *Funny Girl* and sang to us that *people who need people are the luckiest people in the world.* We protested big issues, but we were still kind, and courteous and respectful, and romantic boys and girls.

'By the 1970s we were in a make love not war mood, if the top 100 songs from those days are any indication...but then you can't listen to those songs anymore, can you?

'Then in the 1980s we had corporate gurus begin telling our workplaces that people are our greatest asset.

'But in the 1990s things started to change.

'People were no longer our greatest asset, technology was. The Internet changed our boundaries. Instead of big fish swimming in a little pond, we became little fish swimming in the *world wide web* and that began to change the way we thought and felt about other people. Real people weren't so essential to our lives and success anymore, because we could always replace them with someone or something else that we could access, via the internet.

'Then, as we grew into the new 21$^{st}$ century our face to face contacts were replaced with so many varieties of electronic social media and its consequent rudeness and voyeurism, masquerading as celebrity, and I guess there's no turning back.

'Smart as you are, I do appreciate you don't really understand what I am saying, Oscar, but I wish you, too, could now enjoy the way life used to be!'

Oscar looked at Grandma but felt no emotion or appreciation of Grandma's tearful face.

'Anyway, Grandma, I've come to tell you my wife and I have ordered a baby!'

'Your *wife*? Oh, of course, sorry, I remember now. After marriage equality things got peculiarly unequal, didn't they? The gay community finally decreed that all marriages could only be single sex. And I suppose the government went along with it because it was so much easier to control everyone that way.

'Oscar can I ask you something? Do they teach kids today the history of my century, and what life was like before this Age of Equality?'

'Grandma, I'm sure you know history is forbidden! It is important to focus on the future. People who want to relive the past are sent to special holding areas. They think they are going on a holiday, and in a way they are. It's just that they never come back.'

'What are you going to call your baby, dear?'

'Well, we are thinking, Seven. This year the government has said all babies have to have names that are numbers from one to ten. Some politician thinks it will be a great way to group people in the future... you know, for army service, construction teams, for political service, health workers, everything basically. Everyone is quite excited because it will really streamline decision-making. Of course, we don't know yet what the people named 'Seven' will have to do, but at least our kid can't blame us if it turns out to be something bad,' Oscar said.

Grandma smiled but Oscar was not intending the comment to be funny.

'Does the breeze from my open window bother you dear?' Grandma asked.

'I have a control that can lower the window. The leaves look lovely out on the trees, I can tell autumn is coming. The roses smell lovely, too, although I can't see any rosebushes out on the grounds.'

'Yes, you are so lucky with the technology here, most even forget this is an underground bunker. They haven't figured out how to control the weather yet, and you are so safe and comfortable down here!'

'How much longer do I have to stay here, do you think, Oscar?'

'Well, it's really a great thing you are doing Grandma, even if it's not your choice!

'Your parents didn't realise they were giving you rare blood, I guess, the same way I don't realise what future Seven will have.

'We got a letter last month Grandma. It was from the government saying they were now getting close to matching your blood with the latest manufactures, but until they have success you'll have to stay here to support the remaining humans who share your rare blood type.'

*'I'm ready to go.' 'I'm READY to go' 'GRANDMA!'*

Delores woke with a start from her cat nap on the lounge. Some children's show was background noise on the TV and little Lily had managed to tie her legs and arms to the sides of the lounge chair using the scarves in her dress-up box.

'I'm ready to go to the park now, Grandma Del!'

Delores looked out of the real window and down at her granddaughter, Lily, in her pink frilly dress.

'Thank God for that!' she smiled.

**'WHEN YOU'RE FINISHED CHANGING – YOU'RE FINISHED!'**

***... Ben Franklin***

## When you're finished changing – you're finished!

Marylou was at the curb anxiously checking her phone. There were still no signs of Bobby -- man or message. She noticed it was already ten to five and her irritation grew even stronger.

They'd been married for 10 years now and life seemed to be getting more and more frustrating. She wasn't comfortable. The continual upheaval of her husband's self-styled entrepreneurship continually left her lost in translation.

At least she had put her foot down with the restaurant. Bobby bought the building for one of his many wide-eyed dreams that hadn't eventuated in the end. Instead, it had threatened to become her nightmare.

On the positive side, he'd actually been excited when she then suggested setting up the restaurant. The building had huge open space, a carpark out the back, a perfect area for the kitchen and plenty of picture windows so people (who were also potential customers) could drive past looking at all their clients happily dining!

Marylou had organised the project. She had registered a new company name, hired the tradesmen to transform the functional space into a creative kitchen, and found interior decorators who turned the drab building into a comfortable but trendy eating house that continued to surprise them both with its success.

Five years later, she was proud of *Finess.* They had a steady clientele, great reviews, and the local press was more friend than foe. Public relations was largely Bobby's achievement, giving him credit where credit is due. He was a constant source of quirky commentary whenever they required it.

'When you're finished changing, you're finished' was the latest line he was credited saying in their local paper. (Bobby liked quoting Ben Franklin and the media never did the research to discover where his quirky quotes originated.)

His enthusiasm must have been super-charged by the latest article because now Bobby had worked up a new menu of vegan delicacies that was the polar opposite to their current (and very popular) 'feed the man meat' menu! She'd learned about this today, not from Bobby, but from the slightly perturbed staff after dropping in earlier to make sure no one had called in sick and to check that all was in order for tonight's shift.

Oh well, it was the usual ...Bobby's ying to her yang. Maybe that's why they were still a team when so many of their friends were breaking apart.

She shuddered to think how the new menu was going to go down with the current clientele. And then another shudder followed as she mused whether there was enough money in the account to fund, yet another, marketing campaign for this new menu.

Her phone made a little snigger, letting Marylou know there was a message and with relief she saw it was from Bobby. Looking down the street she saw his car approaching. Her first impulse was to wait till their eyes locked, then turn and march away but she quickly told herself *grow up!*

Marylou got in the car as Bobby flashed her his winning smile.

'*What* on earth are you thinking, Bobby? Are you trying to drive all our customers away? We can do that a lot easier and cheaper by just announcing we're finished!'

'Now Marylou, you know I don't want to upset you, but you're also falling into that *I'm right and you're an idiot* mentality that is sweeping across society these days,' he patted her knee with one arm while keeping the other on the wheel as he handled the traffic.

'It's important for a restaurant to stay trendy and we might as well change with the trends. Everyone's on about climate change and imagine the press and social media interaction we'll reach by saying we've gone vegan to do our bit to counteract global warming!'

'WHAT! You don't even believe all that scare mongering yourself... human environmental pollution with plastic straws, maybe, but the planet is certainly not going to self-destruct anytime soon!'

'Yeah, yeah it doesn't hurt to have a foot in each camp, though! We make money, some of our meat-eaters will become Joni Mitchell vegans looking at both sides now, and then if it looks like people are missing the meat, we'll gradually change back to adding selected meat dishes down the track.

'We can have an influential dietician support our adding meat to the menu and conveniently get more media coverage again! It will be great PR mileage for helping people understand the importance of all food groups.

'It's a win win all around, Marylou!'

Marylou looked at him and had to smile.

'Well, if you're going to finally make some money you might as well take me on a holiday as part of this latest merry go round. Maybe you can find a vegan cruise ship and mix business with pleasure!'

'With me in your life, it's one constant holiday. You know that!'

As he spoke, Marylou noticed Bobby suddenly changing direction and heading towards the mountains.

'Hey, the restaurant's the other way *and* we open in another hour,' alarm and irritation raising the level of her voice.

'Yeah, it's all ok babe, won't take long, I promise!

'I just want to show you this place that might be good for a neat idea I have.'

Marylou closed her eyes, but smiled.

She changed position, pushed down into the leather car seat and made herself feel comfortable.

**'WITHOUT CONTINUAL GROWTH AND PROGRESS, SUCH WORDS AS IMPROVEMENT, ACHIEVEMENT AND SUCCESS HAVE NO MEANING'**

**... *Ben Franklin***

## Without continual growth and progress, such words as improvement, achievement and success have no meaning

Maddie bent over the wash basket in the searing heat, lazily letting her fingers seek out a garment that was easy to peg out on the line. It was so hot, this first lot would be ready to take down as soon as she finished everything in the basket, she thought to herself.

Little Rose had been singing away at her feet and the silence now made Maddie raise her head in attention, looking for her child. A scream locked in her throat as she saw the child mesmerised by a snake slithering towards her, a few metres away.

Oblivious to the danger, Rosie was now on all fours with her toddler head close to the ground, mimicking the snake, as she inched her way towards it.

Maddie frantically looked for something to stop the snake and the glint of steel from Liam's new axe caught her peripheral vision just as she found her voice and screamed to Rose to move away.

She raced for the axe and a stranger took control of her body, striking the snake with strong measured blows, oblivious to the now dead snake, oblivious to the bloody bits of snake flying towards the stunned face of her daughter, oblivious to the pavement that was serving as her chopping board, until finally the sound of the steel meeting the pavement gradually brought her back to herself.

She grabbed Rose and the security of her mother's arms released an instant torrent of tears in the toddler who was crying, more in relief of having her mummy back from an axe wielding monster, than any perceived danger of the snake. They both looked at the aftermath and already the hot sun was baking the remains into something less dramatic and frightening. Maddie transferred her gaze to Liam's once shiny axe which now lay tarnished with snake guts and bent beyond usefulness after her frantically pounding it into the pavement in her extraordinary adrenalin rush to protect her child.

She felt the sweat trickling down from her armpits inside her summer shift and was unsure whether it was from exertion, or anticipating Liam's reaction when he saw the axe.

She hugged Rosie.

'C'mon button, let's go get cleaned up. Daddy will be home soon.'

Later that night Liam and Maddie lay side by side in bed, like iron soldiers.

'Are you ready to tell me what that was really about?' She spoke to the ceiling. 'It was just an axe, for God's sake.'

Rose had finally fallen asleep after requesting countless cuddles from her mother and father after Liam's long tirade at her mother. Physically and emotionally exhausted, Maddie headed for the bedroom where she had found her husband already prone on the bed, his usually genial face still grim.

'They'll be changing the locks and taking possession the day after tomorrow.

'Roddy said they wanted to make it tomorrow but he *bought* us more time, haha.'

'Roddy, Roddy, Roddy... now do you finally understand that he is not the salt of the earth bloke you think he is! He's a poisonous opportunist and the one that got us into this mess in the first place!'

'You know that's not true Maddie.'

'I do so know that it is true and I'm sick to death of your turning the other cheek every time this guy sets you up for another fall!'

Roddy and Liam had grown up on local properties and had known each other all their lives. Liam had been the one who always excelled at school but he decided to follow the family tradition and stick with the farm while Roddy joined the local bank branch at 16. His family had sold out of the area long ago and now lived further down the coast with other farming folk who had listened to their heads over their hearts. Roddy was now the local bank manager and Liam was a farmer of lost returns.

'What will we do?'

'Well, one thing's for sure, I won't be chopping trees.'

They both smiled through their sadness. It will be okay, Maddie thought to herself. Liam is a good man. She snuggled next to his warm body on the hot night and kept the shiver of what tomorrow might bring at bay. Hope floats.

Liam wanted to stay in the Carrageen area and Maddie wanted to move away. Neither had family they could use as an excuse to either stay or move away, they were their own world. It was one of the reasons Liam wanted to stay in the town... he may no longer own the farm but it was still his anchor.

'Everyone is going to be talking about us. They'll be calling you a failure,' Maddie told him the next day as the reality of packing up their belongings overtook them.

'They'll be saying you should have married Penelope when you had the chance and saved the farm by combining the two properties.'

'But, there's only one problem with that ... I don't think Penelope would have let me bring you along, too!'

'Who cares what people think, or say, anyway? ' Liam asked, as Maddie tossed her head in a show of strength.

'Besides, it's going to be just as bad if we move away. People will whisper behind your back and make up their versions about why you've moved to their town... that's human nature.'

As they packed up their belongings in a home that had served three generations of Craddocks, Maddie cajoled, cried, wheedled and even resorted to the emotional blackmail of providing Rose with a better future somewhere else, but Liam held strong and 24 hours later they walked out of the door of their farmhouse, for the last time.

Liam wisely did not tell Maddie that Roddy had provided him with the truck to move their belongings. She needed an enemy to deal with this current disaster, and far better that she vented that on Roddy than become bitter inside. If he had told her about the truck, her pride would have insisted they refuse and the truth was, he had no other options.

They sat in the front cab of the truck, Rose tucked into Maddie's seatbelt, and headed for the town centre, and Liam's new caretaker job that came with very little pay, but a small apartment.

Liam had organised to become the caretaker of a property that Maddie had helped to save through her women's committee. How ironic life is, she thought to herself. She saved Bruce House and now, it was saving her. She cringed when she considered what Mollie Dryden and Wanda More would be saying about her, now. She had endured their snobbish commentary about others before and could just imagine how they would now be gloating on her current misfortune.

Rose jumped out of the truck cab, from her mother's lap into her father's arms and he gently set her on the path to her new house. She felt none of the angst, worry and despair of her parents in the warm summer sunshine that bathed this cottage that would be their new home.

Liam could keep himself occupied with the caretaker demands and duties but in the ensuing weeks Maddie realised she didn't have a clue where to start creating this new life. Her hometown was now the same but entirely different. It was like opening the closet to put on a favourite dress and realising the dress just doesn't fit anymore!

She wasn't sure if it was her pride, or their embarrassment, but women she had considered friends before they lost the farm were now strangers, there was no other way to describe it. Life had changed. They smiled and chatted to her, but it was all somehow insincere and patronizing.

Maddie was always on the farm with Liam and had never had a 'real job'. He didn't say anything but they both silently agreed it would be useful if she could get some part-time work in town.

Rose was confident and happy and so it was like divine intervention when a job came up at the public library that also, fortunately, had a child care centre nearby that could take Rose. The work was simply putting books back where they belonged and doing associated tasks with booking rooms and arranging furniture and refreshments for events and such, but it came with a wage and was surprisingly rewarding, Maddie discovered.

She met Matida and Yaya, Sudanese women with style, heart and fabulous recipes. An introduction to delicious Persian food came from her friendship with Firoozeh, who also told her about

Iran and what it was like coming to Australia where people who knew nothing about her country or experiences, still treated her with suspicion and prejudice.

Matida and Yaya, along with their husbands Clinton and Chriz, and Firoozeh and her husband Habib would join Liam and Maddie at Bruce House every fortnight for a dinner, sharing their life stories and favourite foods in a way Maddie had never experienced when on the farm.

'What a wonderful night,' Maddie said to Liam as they were cleaning up from a night of culinary delights spiced with laughter.

'These people are good people, like us, who have been forced to create new lives for themselves, but they are far richer than the poisonous and pretentious Mollie Dryden, and Wanda More, and that despicable Roddy Rose.'

'Perhaps wealth is not always measured in money,' said Liam as he put his arm over her shoulder and held her close.

'I'm sure Mollie, Wanda and Roddy have some redeeming features, maybe you just have to dig a bit deeper.

'Do we still have a shovel?' He wasn't going to ever let her forget the axe story.

As summer moved into fall, Maddie realised that she had a newfound happiness that felt good.

Firoozeh was becoming a best friend like she had never had before. It was wonderful to hear about another world she had never seen, and would probably never visit other than through Firoozeh's stories. They had wonderful times confiding with each other and discussing the differences and similarities in their lives, family customs, the games they played as kids. Firoozeh was a wonderful seamstress and little Rose loved playing dress-ups with her.

Firoozeh was like Liam, she was always looking for the goodness in people.

Sitting in a coffee shop together, Maddie looked out the window and saw Wanda More walking down the street and muttered 'stupid old cow'.

'Ahh, somewhere in the world, Wanda is considered sacred,' Firoozeh gently chided her.

'I was speaking to Wanda last week. Did you know she lost her only child many years ago, a daughter about nine years old, who died in her arms? Asthma attack.'

Maddie was shocked. 'I have known Wanda for the 15 years since she moved to Carrobeen. She has never mentioned this, nor has anyone else.'

'Sadness is a deep well, everyone copes differently,' said Firoozeh.

'Apparently when she arrived in town she met Roddy Rose and he then helped her establish a research fund in Melbourne. She said that is the only way she can continue on, to have the past life and her present life separate.

'People can be unwittingly cruel. She mentioned that she sends a birthday card to the daughter's best friend every year but they never mention Wanda's daughter in response, it is like she never existed,' Firoozeh said.

'She also said that on the daughter's birthday every year there is an anonymous donation from Carrobeen to the Fund and she knows it is from Roddy.

'They never speak of it, but afterwards when they see each other they have a special hug.

'I thought that was a lovely story because I have always believed in my life there are some things that should only be felt, never spoken,' Firoozeh said softly.

Maddie began to understand how she had misinterpreted the looks Wanda gave to little

Rose. It wasn't that Wanda didn't like children, it was a bittersweet reminder of those lost years.

And Roddy, too, Maddie thought to herself. Perhaps Liam's faith and trust in him isn't misguided and she is the one who has been wrong.

'This news about Wanda makes me feel Liam may be right after all, about Roddy being the salt of the earth,' Maddie confided.

'I've always considered Liam has had this fixation on Roddy just because he's been his best friend since forever, and so he can't see the real Roddy being a loser, like I can.'

'What is this expression 'salt of the earth?' Firoozeh asked. 'Is it unkind, meaning someone is tart, bitter and empty, easily dissolved?'

'No no'. Maddie smiled. 'Quite the opposite'.

'It means someone is trustworthy and kind.'

'Well then, that is an excellent description of Roddy Rose,' Firoozeh said.

'Did you hear that he has helped Matida and Clinton get finance for their church grocery project? Everyone turned them down, so Roddy provided a personal guarantee at his bank for the finance to get them started.

'Apparently his own wife was a little bit cross with him, though,' Firoozeh smiled.

'Matida and Clinton won't let him down,' she said.

'Roddy is such a kind fellow. When we moved over to Bellgrove Street he organised a truck we could use all day at no charge.'

Maddie began to realise why Liam had insisted they call their little girl, Rose, after her mother. It wasn't just a coincidence, like he said at the time, that Rose was also the surname of his best friend.

Later that evening, it was still warm and balmy outside and Rose was tucked up in bed after a full day playing with her new friends at childcare and telling them about her day over dinner.

The grounds of Bruce House were bathed in the pink haze of the waning sunset.

'Let's go sit outside under the mulberry tree and finish our wine,' Maddie said to Liam.

They sat on the park bench and both shared the contented, happy mood that needed no words.

'I have a surprise for you,' said Maddie

'Uh oh, I knew this was too good to be true,' Liam said with a smile and another sip from his glass.

'Look over there, behind the tree,' Maddie said.

He slowly moved over behind the tree and all of a sudden guffawed loudly, holding up his crumpled axe for her to see.

‘I thought I would hang on to it. I was sure it would be useful sooner or later,’ Maddie smiled.

‘It’s time to bury the axe’ she said with a smile as she handed the giftwrapped garden trowel he’d asked her to buy for the flowerbeds.

‘Daylight savings ends soon… I thought we could invite the Roses over too, along with Firoozeh, Matida and Yaya next weekend.’

He gave her a hug.

‘I knew you’d dig deeper’, he said.

Printed in Great Britain
by Amazon

81213775R00102